DA JING

The Fastest Knitter
in the West

Mary Arrigan   Korky Paul

To David Brendan Arrigan
M.A.

For Chloe Duval
K.P.

First published in Great Britain 2002
by Egmont Books Ltd
239 Kensington High Street, London W8 6SA
Text copyright © Mary Arrigan 2002
Illustrations copyright © Korky Paul 2002
The author and illustrator have asserted their moral rights
Paperback ISBN 0 7497 4867 2
10 9 8 7 6 5 4 3 2 1
A CIP catalogue record for this title is available from the British Library
Printed in Dubai

Contents

Red Bananas

DARNED DUST

Jemima Jinglebob lived in the town of Buckaroo, way out in the Wild West. Nothing much ever happened in Buckaroo. In fact the only thing the people of Buckaroo ever complained about was the dust that blew in from the desert.

'Darned dust,' they said. 'It makes our town right dirty.'

Gets in our hair.

Jemima Jinglebob's pa was big. He was as broad as a brick wall and hairier than a buffalo. His skin was rougher than old iron.

My pa is as strong as an ox!

His hands are like shovels.

Jemima wished her pa would go hunting for bears and shoot holes in ace cards. She wished he would round up mean outlaws who wore mucky boots and had no manners. She wished he would do all the things that rootin' tootin' men of the West did.

But no, Pa Jinglebob wasn't interested in any of those things. Pa Jinglebob liked to knit. He knitted the finest woolly jumpers in the West.

Day after day he rocked back and forth on the porch in his big wooden rocker, knitting.

Jemima wished the people of Buckaroo would stop sniggering whenever they passed by and saw him. But Pa didn't mind. 'One plain, one purl,' he'd say.

Jemima sighed and went out to practise lassoing the boys who jeered at Pa.

One day a shout went up from the town lookout.

'There's a horse comin' in,' he roared. 'He's a-gallopin' and a-sweatin'.'

Everyone ran to see. The sweaty rider jumped off his horse. He took a mouthful of water from the horse trough and spat it out. 'There's trouble a-comin' folks,' he said. 'Not-Nice Nellie and her Bandits are headed this way!'

Everyone gasped.

NOT-NICE NELLIE!

'We've got to have a sheriff,' said the mayor, who didn't want to be in charge when Not-Nice Nellie hit town. 'We need a sheriff who'll clap that dame in the clink. Who'd like to be sheriff?'

The townspeople looked at their feet and began to mutter.

Mr. Grace the saloon keeper was busy.

I have to squash some lemons for the lemonade . . .

The undertaker was busy.

All the cowboys were busy.

'Someone has to be sheriff,' wailed the mayor. 'We can't have bandits coming in here willy-nilly and no sheriff to put manners on them.'

'I'll do it,' said Pa Jinglebob. 'I'll be sheriff.'

'You!' everyone laughed. 'What a joke! A sheriff who knits woolly jumpers?'

But the mayor was so relieved that he immediately pinned the sheriff's star on Pa.

'Okay, Pa Jinglebob,' he said. 'You're officially sheriff. Now, excuse me, I have to see to . . . something in my wardrobe.'

Jemima's heart nearly burst with pride when she looked at her pa's badge.

That's my brave pa!

BANDITS
IN BUCKAROO

It wasn't long before hooves were heard thundering in the distance.

'Get your gun, Sheriff,' shouted everyone, before running into their houses to hide.

'No need for guns,' said Sheriff Jinglebob, wiping the dust off his new badge with his woolly sleeve.

'But Pa, you must use your gun,' said Jemima. 'You are the sheriff and that's what sheriff's do.'

Pa shook his head and tucked his knitting into his pocket. 'Guns are for wallies,' he said. 'I ain't afraid of a bunch of gun-totin' wallies.'

But even he had to admit that Not-Nice Nellie was the most fearsome person he'd ever seen.

She galloped into town, shouting rudely and shooting at passing clouds with her noisy rifle.

'Get out here, you mean bunch of cowards,' she screamed. 'Or I'll knock down every darned house and grind your miserable bones to dust.'

Scared of such a loud lady the townspeople crawled out from under their stairs and behind their wardrobes.

'Do something, Sheriff,' they muttered.

'Do something, Pa,' said Jemima.

Grind down our bones?

Heck! How would we get about?

But before he had time to think, Not-Nice Nellie and her hollerin' Bandits had rounded everyone up.

'Get down that hole,' she said, pointing to the old dried-up well at the edge of town.

'Now look here, my good woman,' said
Mrs Grace, who kept her husband's saloon
neat and tidy and smelling of lavender polish.
'You can't just dump a whole townful of
people into a hole.'

'Oh yeah?' snarled Not-Nice Nellie.
'Watch me, sunshine.'

With that, she and her Bandits pushed
everyone into the smelly dried-up well.
Jemima felt her cheeks and ears blush with
shame when folks began to grumble at Pa.

'Might as well have elected a grizzly bear,'
said the mayor.

Jemima stamped her foot and frowned.
'Don't you mind them, Pa,' said Jemima.
'I think you're smashing.'

Pa smiled and took out his knitting. 'One
plain, one purl,' he said.

'Oh, Pa,' groaned Jemima.

ROTTEN VARMINTS

By now it was dark. All that could be heard was the noisy shouting and laughing of Not-Nice Nellie and her Bandits as they raided the town. That and the click–click of Pa's knitting needles as he knitted one plain, one purl. People were quiet, mainly because Jemima had promised to flatten the next person who said one word about her pa.

'Listen to that,' gasped Miss Brown, the schoolteacher. 'They're smashing the desks in the schoolroom.'

'Great!' said twenty young voices in the dark.

'Now they're taking the corks out of my lemonade,' said Mr Grace. 'Listen to those corks pop.'

'The rotten varmints!' said the same twenty voices.

They're frying Mrs Grace's sausages!

Smell that!

Not my home-made sausages!

'It's all Pa Jinglebob's fault,' muttered someone in the corner. 'A decent sheriff would have clapped Not-Nice Nellie in the clink.'

'I told you not to say bad things about my pa,' said Jemima.

ANOTHER HAIRY OLD JUMPER?

Now the moon was shining down the old well. It lit up the faces of the folks of Buckaroo who were huddling scared and cold. It lit up the flash of Pa Jinglebob's knitting needles. It lit up the frown on Jemima's face.

'There! All done,' said Pa Jinglebob, snapping the wool with his great big teeth.

'What's all done, Pa?' asked Jemima. 'Another hairy old jumper?'

'Nope,' said Pa.

A jumper ... pah!

Then he shook out the
thing he'd been knitting. There was
a loud gasp of amazement.

'A ladder!' people cried. 'Pa Jinglebob's
gone and knitted us a ladder.'

'Time to teach Not-Nice Nellie and her
bunch a lesson,' said Pa.

He handed Jemima the top of the ladder.

'Tie this to the tree, honeybun,' he said. And then he threw his little daughter right up out of the old well. As she tied the woolly ladder to the tree, Jemima could hear the Bandits hootin' and hollerin'.

'Pa will fix you lot,' she said to herself.

Puffing and panting, Pa Jinglebob hauled himself up the ladder. Then he did a very strange thing.

'Hey!' shouted the mayor. 'Why arc you pulling up the ladder, Sheriff Jinglebob?'

'You'd get in my way,' Pa Jinglebob yelled back.

So long, folks!

By the light of the moon, Jemima and her pa crept into town. What a sight met their eyes! There in the saloon, drinking every last drop of lemonade, sat Not-Nice Nellie and her Bandits. And what a noise they were making, dancing on the tables and belching rudely, without even saying, 'Excuse me.'

On the floor were two big bags with the word LOOT printed on them.

'They've nicked all the cash in town,' said Pa. 'Now that's *real* bad.'

There was worse. On the picture of the mayor there were squashed tomatoes where his eyes should be have been.

On the stairs four of the Bandits were having a pillow fight. The feathers from the ripped pillows stuck to everything especially to the broken eggs that dripped down the wall.

I just love this lemonade!

Who turned out the light?

LOOT

Not-Nice Nellie was
throwing half-eaten
sausages into the air
and shooting them.

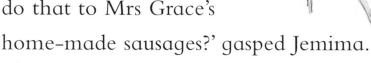

'How can anyone
do that to Mrs Grace's
home-made sausages?' gasped Jemima.

'These are dangerous people,' said Pa.

Then he smiled and took out his knitting
needles. 'I have a plan,' he said. 'Listen up,
sweet Jemima.'

RIP-ROARIN' FUN

A short while later, Jemima Jinglebob crawled under the swing doors of the saloon. None of the Bandits noticed the small girl. They were too busy messing up Mrs Grace's good saloon.

Jemima frowned her deepest frown and stamped her foot.

'Get your hands up,' she shouted.

Nobody heard. They just went on with their rip-roarin' fun.

'I SAID PUT YOUR HANDS UP!' Jemima roared.

The noise stopped. The Bandits turned to see who was giving orders. How they howled when they saw little Jemima standing with her hands on her hips.

'Get down from Mrs Grace's polished tables, you scruffy varmints,' growled Jemima. 'And come quietly.'

For five whole minutes the Bandits fell about laughing. Wiping the tears of laughter from her eyes, Not-Nice Nellie peered at Jemima.

'Say, kid,' she said. 'Who knitted your jumper?'

'My pa knitted it,' replied Jemima.

'Her pa knitted it!' How the Bandits laughed again.

'Who's your pa?' asked Not-Nice Nellie when she could catch her breath.

'He's the sheriff,' said Jemima proudly.

The sheriff is a sissy knitter.

Now that really made the Bandits double up and roll around the floor.

'Oh lawksy me!' gurgled Not-Nice Nellie. 'The sheriff of plain and purl! I didn't think it would be this easy to take over the town of Buckaroo.'

They shrieked and giggled, the rotten lot. They hollered and sniggered. But Jemima just smiled. Pa had told her that this was the very moment to do her important bit. Reaching out, she whipped up one of the bags marked LOOT.

Got it!

LOOT

'I'm taking this dough,' she shouted, just before running out the door. That certainly brought Not-Nice Nellie and her Bandits to their senses, those who had any.

'Quick! She's got our good loot!' they cried. 'After her!'

Jumping down from the tables, they pushed and shoved one another as they chased after brave Jemima Jinglebob.

And that was just what Jemima wanted.

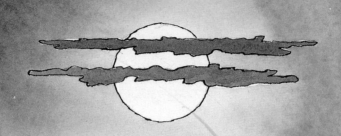

BRAVE HEROES

Around by the general store Jemima led the roaring mob of rude Bandits. By the light of the moon she crossed the street to the forge. Glancing back to see that they were following, she ran inside.

'We've got her now!' shouted the Bandits. 'You're cornered, kid.'

Get the kid!

Still pushing and shoving one another, they galloped into the forge. Big mistake.

Stretched across the forge, from one side to the other, was a huge woolly web, beautifully knitted, one plain and one purl.

'Gotcha!' hollered Sheriff Jinglebob as the scruffy mob got tangled in the hairy threads. Then he threw a knitted net over the lot and, with Jemima's help, trapped Not-Nice Nellie and her bunch of Bandits. How they roared.

'Now who's a sissy sheriff?' said Jemima. 'My pa is the cleverest, toughest sheriff in the whole West.'

Hee Hee.

'Aw, shucks!' said Pa Jinglebob, blushing under his stubbly beard.

'You let us out of this woolly net,' said Not-Nice Nellie. 'This is not funny!'

'Yes it is,' laughed Jemima, 'I'm having a whole heap of fun.'

Pa and Jemima Jinglebob dragged the netted Bandits across the street and pushed them into the clink.

Then they went back to the old well and let the ladder down.

'Where are they?' asked the mayor, looking nervously around as he emerged from the well. 'Where are Not-Nice Nellie and her bunch?'

'In the clink,' said Jemima proudly. 'My brave pa and I captured them and dumped them in the clink.'

'On your own?' asked Mister Grace, who was next to emerge.

'Yep,' said Jemima.

'Amazing,' said Mrs Grace. 'What a pair of brave heroes.'

Later on a loud shrieking sound echoed through the town. It caused a couple of bald eagles to collide in mid-air and fall into the trough. It spooked every horse in Buckaroo.

What in the heck was that?

'What now!' Jemima exclaimed, rushing outside. Mrs Grace was storming up the street, followed by the rest of the townsfolk. She had just seen the mess in the saloon!

'Trouble, Pa!' said Jemima, running in to warn the sheriff.

'Yup,' said Pa Jinglebob.

'Aren't you going to do something.'

'Maybe,' grunted Pa. 'One plain, one purl.'

Mrs Grace clomped across the sheriff's office and pushed her angry face close to Pa Jinglebob's. 'Gimme the keys, Sheriff,' she hollered. 'So's I can deal with that scruffy prisoner and her bunch of layabouts.'

And with that she slapped the sheriff's desk so hard that everyone jumped. Except Pa Jinglebob who kept on muttering, 'One plain, one purl.'

Jemima ran to protect her pa from the fury of Mrs Grace.

'Out of the way, kid,' yelled Mrs Grace. 'I'm madder than a prairie dog with pimples on his paws.'

'Do something, Pa,' said Jemima. 'Mrs Grace is fightin' mad and things could get out of hand.'

'One plain, one purl,' said Pa Jinglebob.

'Oh Pa,' groaned Jemima. But before she could finish the groan, her pa stood up.

'There's a nice lot o' knittin',' he said, holding up a bundle of stripy squares.

'KNITTIN'?' shouted Mrs Grace. 'I got more on my mind than knittin'!'

He's done it again!

'Hold on to your garters, Missus,' said Pa Jinglebob calmly, handing the bundle of knitted squares to the red-faced Mrs Grace.

'These squares will sort out that rowdy lot. This is what you must do.'

And as he explained, Mrs Grace's face smoothed back from furious red to cheery pink.

Amazing.

Mrs Grace reached through the bars and handed the knitted squares to Not-Nice Nellie.

'Cleaning cloths,' she said. 'You lot get out there and clean up or Pa Jinglebob will knit scratchy woollen cages and shove you in them.'

'Yes, Ma,am,' muttered Not-Nice Nellie and her Bandits, looking fearfully at Pa Jinglebob and his knitting needles.

'One plain, one purl,' Pa sighed.

Mrs Grace stood over Not-Nice Nellie and her boys as they cleaned up the town. In fact they became so good at it, they set up a cleaning business right there in Buckaroo. Nellie made out a big sign that said,

NICE NELLIE'S
Neat 'n' Tidy Cleaning Company
Walls and Floors Scrubbed
Shiny Stuff Polished
Carpets Thumped
Cowboys Hosed
Fleas Banished

We're in business!

Peace returned to the town. Jemima Jinglebob watched the other kids' fathers making a mighty fuss as they set off to hunt bears.

'Fat chance of catching a bear with all that hootin' and hollerin',' she said. She smiled and looked proudly at her pa as he sat on the porch muttering, 'One plain, one purl.'

'That's my brave pa,' she said. 'He can catch just about anything, when he wants to. My pa is the fastest knitter in the West.'

And nobody argued with that.

The End